LOST BETWEEN LIGHT & SHADOW

A Collection of Dark Poetry

C. H. LINDSAY, EDITOR

ISBN: 978-1-952043-17-8

Library of Congress Control Number: 2024933552

Edited by C. H. Lindsay

Cover designed by C. Lindsay Carlisle

Cover Art by Darkmoon Art on Pixabay.com

LOST BETWEEN LIGHT & SHADOW

Contents

Branches and Bone
C.R. Langille

There is a patch of woods, nestled in a forgotten place
Where fools will wander only to disappear without a
trace
When the wind blows soft, the trees will creak and moan
Followed by the snap and crack of branches and bone

Deep in the darkest timber, where the trees tower high
The shadows dance a slow waltz with the moon in
the sky
They wait in hunger as their stomachs grumble and groan
A frenzied madness with the crack of branches and bone

So don't go wandering through the forest at night
For they hide in the gloom with a gluttonous delight
Now they salivate like hounds, their next meal is shown
And they move silent, except for the crack of branches
and bone

I'm Forty-Fifth
Inna V. Lyon

When my body in the closed casket
arrives in my dear hometown.
I will lose my grip on time and start asking
if, from there, my only way is down.

Down to earth, where the worms and the larvae
will provide for my body's death warrant.
Down to earth, where souls are starving
for someone to bring justice to the fallen.

The Russian priest with the cross boldly shown
will be standing in cold autumn showers.
And my mother, for count unknown,
will be fainting in black head cover.

Gun salutes by the uniformed members
spook civilians with gut-wrenching fears.
Paper cups in the man's hand trembling,
passing vodka half-mixed with tears.

The official—drunken with eyes bulging—
one who worships bloodthirsty Putin—
tells heart-breaking statistics: "This solder's
the forty-fifth killed in active duty."

Forty-fifth for this small of a town.
Forty-fifth in the row of the fallen.

From now on, I will only fall down.
From now on, my life's a whiff of tree pollen.

Messy Leavings
Lillian Angelovic

handfuls of colorful gel pens
paperclips in a pill bottle
crystallized honey
cat hair
the neighbor's condescending scowl
an hourglass
peppermint tea
drums keeping the beat
the sister who can't quite interact appropriately in any situation
mud
there's the charging cable
sewing pins stuck in a red cushion
loud guitars
rocks that were interesting when I picked them up
a watch with a dead battery
glue sticks
last year's art calendar
the sister whose childhood self looked up to me
citrus-scented body wash
a headache
empty Amazon boxes
the horror in her eyes
an old poem that needs more work
hairpins
blood
the sister whose suicide attempt earned appropriate therapy

sparkly red ribbon
these look like painkillers
et tu Brute?

David C. Kopaska-Merkel

the swimmer's bones
settle to the mound—
mermaids' bellies full

the leviathan
Kevin Wasden

in the fading twilight
    in my own dimming twilight
i face the sea
    she beckons return to me

shoulders stooped fingers gnarled
        i struggle into the canoe
beside me my wife places a basket
        woven by her hands and filled with dried fruits
            a gesture of love
    i thank her
            devotion expressed in sustenance
                the last of herself she is able to give
                the last I am able to receive

with a quiet smile
    i hold my wife
            touch her cheek and bid farewell
            she understands
            a silent knowing
    she stands strong
            tears run dry

my son
    a tower of chiefly strength
        guides my boat to the waiting waves
they all watch
    my wife

my son
        the village
as i slowly
        ever so slowly
                row toward the boundless sea

beneath the moon
        pulling tides pulling me
                i stop far from land

we've always feared the leviathan's might
        avoiding waters where he roams
but today i sing his name aloud
        calling him to me
                the great destroyer

he emerges
        a force of nature
spray and fury
        jaws agape
his colossal presence overwhelms
        i draw near
                arms extended toward my fate

with a tender descent
        we meld
                into the watery abyss
                        we venture forward
                                bound together
                        the leviathan and i
                        a journey into the embrace of the divine

House of the Fundead
Skye Caden

There are some dreams worth living in
That wish for days which could have been,
A world where every rule can bend
And playtime never has to end.
A lingering calliope
Will whisper its cacophony
One night each year, when darkness falls,
To those who listen for its calls.
That lilting tune in stagnant air,
It carries from a funny fair,
Where neon casts an eerie gleam
Through fog produced by no machine.
The grounds are packed with games and treats,
Each stall stuffed sick with sticky sweets;
A carousel of apparitions
Spins a spell of superstitions.
The center tent is filled with cheers
But looks worn well beyond its years;
With faded stripes all torn and stained
Its pallid patchwork seems restrained.
Performers join you for your jaunt,
With toothy grins and features gaunt
And masks of paint like polished bone;
They promise you won't be alone.
And in the back, a house of mirrors
Inspires wonder, heightens fears.
It shrinks and stretches each dimension
'Till you're lost in your reflection.

You wander through the dizzy lights —
The glowing hues of showy sights —
Beset by soothing memory,
One night becomes a century
For of the denizens, not one
Has seen the circus flee the sun,
And none of them can end their story,
Stuck in festive purgatory…

Aftermath
C. H. Lindsay

Dawn bleeds through rain-dense clouds,
    igniting virga into liquid fire:
an omen of evanescence.

Green mist shimmers in the tainted light
    as it hovers over swollen rivers,
pregnant with icy Spring.

City remnants rise from sullied waters:
    sentinels of stone and steel.
The solitary legacy of man's demise.

Rocky mountains observe quiescently;
    preserve history in mud and stone.
Await the next evolution.

A Gravestone
K. Scott Forman

A forest
Light seeping through leaves
Their quivering reminds him of the ocean
Reminds him of her
He bends down to put his face against the damp stone
Kisses it
Rubs it clockwise counting to thirty

For all their years of marriage

Nebrit
Talysa Sainz

In the town of Nebrit
No one dares venture out
under a full moon,
for that's when
moonshadows come to life.
They are cast by a phantom of sunlight,
an estranged echo of the celestial glow,
and emboldened by the lunar light.
The shadows arise from the earth
and wreak havoc on their hosts.

Wicked monsters they are,
full of dark deeds
and darker minds,
prone to twist souls—
lovers into fighters
rational to wild,
cautious into reckless—
or simply take over their bodies
with such shadiness
their souls are unsalvageable.

When the moon is full,
the town descends into blackness.
Curtains close, doors lock,
the streets are vacated,
and the townspeople hide.
Except for one.

darling and fierce Lily Amaris,
born in full moonlight
and grown twenty years
as the untouchable.

She emerges at midnight,
dances with dusk,
and twirls through twilight.

Some say she tamed her moonshadow,
she's already corrupted,
or she isn't human.
No one asks, but they all tell stories,
trying to figure out
if her magic is made of
darkness or light.

Sentiments and Snacks
Elizabeth Suggs

Today is a day for myself—
The hungry beast within my soul.
I feed it crackers and thoughts and nightmares.

The Divine Crow
Jonathan Reddoch

I was born in a tree
But from the bough I fell

And broke my knees
And cracked my shell

I have two hidden eyes
But neither to see

I have ebony wings
But mustn't flee

I stalk the living
Hoping they die

I haunt the shadow
Of the fly

Clasp your hands
And hope to prey

The Crow your soul
To peck away

The Stalking
Inspired by Edgar Allen Poe's *The Bells*
Greg R. Goodman

See the corn in tidy rows!
Golden rows!
What a world of nourishment each yellow kernel stows!
Look how it grows and grows and grows
You know, it's really such a sight
In morning light, they seem to twinkle
When irrigation starts to sprinkle
As they drink to their delight
Looking fine, fine, fine
In a circular design
Through those trials and tribulations
that the farmer so well knows
There in rows, rows, rows, rows
Rows, rows, rows —
From the sowing to the growing of the rows

II

See the ears lined up in rows
All the rows!
What a world of sustenance their energy bestows
Through the summer, day and night
Watch them grow, what a delight!
To go from seeds to stalks then shuck
It just takes time
What a genius stroke of luck
That this veggie feeds so many

for a buck
It's sublime
And as everybody knows
It's a rush to eat the veggie, growing in the rows!
But suppose…
Just suppose,
There are secrets, in the rows
Hidden secrets in repose
Children playing in the swaying
Of the rows, rows, rows
In the rows, rows, rows, rows
rows, rows, rows
Children's laughter ever after in the rows

III

Feel the breathing of the rows
Living rows!
What a tale of terror, in the
horrifying rows!
Always starting late at night
How they scream from out of sight
Missing children that can't speak
They only shriek, shriek, shriek
Out of tune!
We, in clamorous appealing to the mercy of God's will
In a mad expostulation "It's the children who will kill"
You see, for them it's just a thrill
If they're not stopped, our blood will spill
It's their resolute endeavor
To kill us, now or never
Then drag the bodies at full moon
To the rows, rows, rows!
What a tale their terror shows!

What despair!
How they stalk, and slash! What gore!
It's a horror they outpour
In the subtle moonlit glow that fills the air
It's the ears that drive assaults
Through extolling
And controlling
They say "the danger is adults"
Then each undead child knows
Through cajoling
And controlling
How they must obey the rows!
They're obeying and fulfilling all the
anger of the rows!
Of the rows!
Of the rows, rows, rows, rows
Rows, rows, rows —
There's a shocking evil stalking in the rows

IV

Hear the chanting from the rows
Undead rows!
Sending chills into the air
Their monody in lows
We all wonder every night
Who'll be missing at first light
Oh, the melancholy menace of that verse!
From the rows, hear the notes
Shrieking sounds straight from their throats
It's a curse
And the children— undead children
Who are dwelling in the rows
all perverse

They start killing, killing, killing
And you know what's even worse
Is the fact that they are willing
And they don't appear averse
To consuming other children
For they are no longer human
They are ghouls
At dawn, their king then calls
And he calls, calls, calls
Calls
For a pæan from the rows
And his evil grinning grows
With the pæan from the rows
And the wicked fervor grows
Keeping time, time, time
In a ghoulish kind of rhyme
To the pæan of the rows
Of the rows
Keeping time, time, time
A macabre kind of rhyme
To the swaying of the rows
Of the rows, rows, rows—
To the preying in the rows
Keeping time, time, time
As the shrieking really flows
In a morbid sort of rhyme
Undead children in the rows
In the rows, rows, rows—
We dread children in the rows
In the rows, rows, rows, rows
Rows, rows, rows—
Hear the slurping and the burping in the rows!

Lorraine Schein

ghost taxi driver
knows the fastest routes
through corpse traffic

My Undead Neighbor
Joshua P. Sorensen

When I see my neighbor,
It fills me up with dread.
I see him only in the night.
He's one of the undead.
Maybe he's a Zombie
That shuffles down the street,
Hunting little children
To eat their bones and meat.
Or a cursed Vampire
With fangs and pale white skin.
Remember, if he knocks
I'll never let him in.
Perhaps a ghostly Specter,
Floating through the air.
Whose body has long rotted,
Including his long hair.
My parents often scold me
And tell me it ain't true.
No one lives next door;
Although I often view
That neighbor watching me,
When it's very dark.
Then he smiles brightly,
His teeth just like a shark
And so, I'm very careful.
Don't go out when it is late.
Keep waiting for the sunlight,
When everything is great!

Siren's Sorrow
C.R. Langille

Her voice floats across the waves like a gull
Hooks my soul like some lovestruck fool
She cuts the water like a shark, her eyes hungry
Into the drink I go, her song fades away
A deluge of tears falls, saltier than the sea
Realization crashes against rocky shores
Dragged down into the great dark fathoms
I claw for the surface; my fingers grasp only hope
Flimsy insubstantial, only for fools and romantics
Her embrace, cold and tight, not warm like she promised
Claws rip and tear with abandon, my heart and soul
I am but food for the deep

The Mirror Cracked
Greg R. Goodman

Walking alone, the pines bend and sway
in a rising wind, catching my attention.
The trees move irreverently,
like they're laughing at me,
limbs holding onto jiggling bellies,
shoulders shaking, fingers pointing.

Birds in sheltered solidarity, hiding
among the trees, twitter mellifluous secrets
to each other…thinking I won't hear.
The clamor intensifies,
penetrating every recess of my being,
amplifying the angst.

I self-consciously quicken my pace,
but in the gathering storm, I lose the path.
Thick underbrush tugs at my clothing
like hundreds of hands, reaching out
from every level of Dante's imagination,
trying to pull me into the inferno.

My feet feel heavy. The terrain
is unstable and constantly shifting,
like I'm in a nightmare, unable to run.
I realize I'm mired in the remains of
the other troubled souls who
ventured this way and were consumed.

I feel their eyes upon me, willing me
into their world. Sinking and fearing
inundation, I reach for an overhanging
branch. The limb, polished smooth
by the agony of other encounters,
offers no quarter, my burden, too much…

Devolving to Grayscale
C. H. Lindsay

Sun seeps over the horizon
heralding yet another day
as sky changes from charcoal to
pewter in its never-ending
rotation: a once-bright azure
faded to soulless emptiness.
Slate frogs languish among steel-toned
waterlilies and ashen trees.
Pallid ravens lurk overhead,
drift desultorily and watch
evolution's once-bright array
progressively dissolve into
achromatic sterility
and death-like desaturation.

Comfort to Know
Jonathan Reddoch

It must be a comfort

To know

The day you'll die

Hung

By the neck

For stealing

A chicken

To feed

Your starving children

January 15

1457

They will live

Because you died

Devour Like Sharks
Brian Mealing

I see purple and blue rainbows in the dark
Like giant claws in a wave upon the shore
My weapons cannot hurt these rainbows
The iridescence is a trap
Two colors; two creatures
This pair of spirits
Haunted ghosts and zombies
They sneak to me like shadows
I run; I dash
They chase; they catch
Then devour like sharks
The rainbows are still hungry

I Was Troubled
Lillian Angelovic

Sadness radiates down my arms
and finding no escape
returns to infect my heart.

It came to pass, or to stay
to dream alone
who will comfort my sleep?

In the morning I call for the magicians
but there is no venom to extract
from this troubled spirit.

Only a cry, a prayer
ill at ease each day
who can interpret?

Look out to me, Lord
from the cloud and the pillar of fire
sore troubled in the dark.

Forty years, more
wounds gaping unseen
whose sin hath beset me?

Here now is the blood evidence
the sweet smoke of sacrifice
filling the temple courtyard.

Washed but still afflicted, cursed
my soul quakes
what pain rends this veil?

David C. Kopaska-Merkel

Jack rises
from the midnight field—
moon-wide grin

The Ghost of My Room
Joshua P. Sorensen

The heater blows like a furnace
But the air even now chills
My bones quake inside
Icy flesh
Breath frosts
No human specter
Or vengeful wraith
Each occupant over decades
Pieces of life, bits of spirt
Tiny artifacts
The room tires of life
Each new person brings warmth
But then they abandon it
And now the atmosphere
Lies dead and cold

Sophie's Lantern
Jonathan Reddoch

The world of chaos resides just beyond the borders
Of our mundane vision
Ancient felines, night wolves, and a select few humans
Have the flickering sight to perceive it

Fewer still have the mental stamina
To fathom its aggressive appetite
Yet a single soul maintains the fortitude
To deny the soothing embrace of the dark void

Sophie Smith carries within her a soft beacon
That illuminates the immediate otherworld
Weakly pressing the umbra back
She feels the ever-present shadows reaching in

Always encroaching
Breaching our dimension
So near they can taste it:
Her joyful spirit

Should she ever allow her fragile beam to dim
The dark maw will claw in
Devouring her and…
Everything in the direct vicinity of our local universe

Can Sophie's lantern save us forever from incursion?
So much darkness knocking at our door
All it takes to end our reality

Is one mere melancholic day for our lowly savior

Do not forsake all hope
Not just yet
Sophie has light enough
To endure the darkness--even if ours goes out

flaming wings of dreams
Linda M. Crate

i have always felt caught
between the teeth of
light and darkness,

my mother is a goddess
of light pure and holy;
my father is a monster
of darkness and blight—

it makes me wonder at times
if i am a sacred thing,
or just a softer shade
of evil;

perhaps i am both light and darkness—

the past is always haunting me:
faces i do not know
dancing in my periphery,
flying through my dreams;

i grow weary of chasing nightmares,
and only wish to hold onto the flaming
wings of dreams.

Lorraine Schein

to hail a late-night taxi
I wave a black shroud
for the ghost driver

The Rocking Horse
Kevin Wasden

in the corners of attics
old things are lost
forgotten
forsaken
and time
                        counted in layers of dust
ceases
until a curious boy
enters in
reigniting time
rekindling hope
the old rocking horse
awakes and recalls
            the boy on its back
                    to and fro
                    cowboys and rodeos
giggles and companionship
then echoes a mother's call
time
for the boy to leave
time
cruelly flowing silent and swift
time
stealing away time
and the pain
                        of loneliness
                        of insignificance
                        of nothingness

                returns
and the wooden toy
summoning a modicum of life
sways
a small teeter
witnessed
in the corner of a young boy's eye
who stops
who sees the old wooden horse
        in the dark corner of the attic
who smiles
and for an infinite moment
remembers

Grave Thinking
Greg R. Goodman

I move among mental gravestones,
my recalcitrant memorials
to the festering.
Some are worn smooth
like a worry stone.
Others remain angular and acute,
still sharp and unfinished,
like caustic personalities.

I come here often
to rummage through the past.
The captive traveler
in this temporal chasm-
consumed with grievance
disadvantaged by circumstance,
fallen from relevance-
in search of quietus.

Upon opening this sepulcher,
a disquieting thrum permeates me —
the heartbeat of the chimera.
Born of another dimension,
its existence is foreign,
yet it survives only within me.
Like a parasite, it nourishes itself
on self, demanding I return to feed it.

My thoughts race.

Intransigent memories of
painful transgressions hover
over me like circling vultures.
All seek satisfaction through
absolution, inurement or death.
I struggle for closure,
but this portal's become unhinged.

I realize now that each pilgrimage
empowers the beast, adding angst
rather than resolution.
The result is a toxic residue that
clings to me like wet clothing.
I long for release, but find I'm tethered,
dreading the next visit, like a
bad dog waiting to be beaten again.

So persist the ancient demons
that serve this world.
These timeless specters lurk
in the shadows, without satisfaction.
They are the guardians of this temple,
who maintain the facade and
stoke the fires, keeping it fresh
for my inevitable return.

Funeral Tolling
Lillian Angelovic

"Never think that war, no matter how necessary nor how justified, is not a crime. Ask the infantry and ask the dead."
—Ernest Hemingway, *For Whom the Bell Tolls*

My thin body naked
I fled to you, dripping from the shower, knowing you were safety
Never questioned, as a mother's love
I forgot the childhood trauma so you remind me
Recorded in your journal all along, next to what I said and who was there
Never mentioned, clasped tightly in a mother's arms

A dirt clod
I don't fit the words now, the story you tell, the reality I cannot see
Never prominent but hidden underground, a filthy secret
I dig and rake and only weeds grow
Something must be wrong with me or you would share more than hello, a look like a smile
Never uncovering the growing doom

The enemy
I must know you love me because you haven't killed me yet
Always marred, set aside by my father
I learned to recognize his rejection every day

Then your face twists with hidden anger and the last word
Always recollectable now, a memory scar

Neighbors, sisters, brothers
All about saw my state and tolled the bell
Never speaking as the lamp slowly dimmed
I expected it, had no idea, cannot comprehend the sound
Questioning reality does not heal the sick who don't know to listen
Never hearing, shrouded behind the curtain

The wood floor
I look down to avoid faces and see only the chandelier
Not angry but mortified
I did not predict bombers overhead, disconcerted by friendly fire and fratricide, a rout
Ringing in my ears narrows vision but I know the rule
Not to live for torture, but to seek death first

Bridges destroyed
I wait for the muffled knell, the quiet roar of water washing me away
Always wondering which of us was the fascist
And did we find it out
Where you will go I will go too, when the peals finish
Always remembering I am your child

Autumn Autumn
Zeeshan Shahzad

Autumn, oh Autumn, with colors so bold,
You paint the world in hues, a sight to behold.
Leaves cascade gracefully, in red and gold,
Whispering tales, as your gentle breeze unfolds.

As days grow shorter, and nights turn cold,
Your beauty empowers, a story untold.
With each step we take, on paths of old,
We delight in the crunch, of leaves, so bold.

In nature's embrace, magic weaves its spell,
Pumpkins on porches, apples we pluck and sell.
The harvest moon rises, our spirits swell,
Around fires we gather, with loved ones to dwell.

Cinnamon fills the air, with its sweet allure,
As we gather together, our hearts feel secure.
Golden sunsets paint the sky, shades of orange pure,
A moment of tranquility, forever to endure.

In your presence, solace and respite we find,
Autumn, oh Autumn, you instill belief in our mind.
As time passes, and seasons unwind,
Under your glow, comfort, not strangeness, we find.

Autumn, oh Autumn, a season for reflection,
A time for appreciation, a heartfelt connection.

In our minds your beauty shall never perish,
In our hearts, your essence we'll ever cherish.

Godless Society
C. H. Lindsay

Sunset burns crimson red,
bleeding through broken clouds
onto a world bereft
of Asgard's care. Midgard
wakens elsewhere, fed through
Bifrost's umbilical.
Valhalla's reward gone—
lost by the unfaithful—
leaving mankind destined
for their own Ragnarök.

Penpals?
Joshua P. Sorensen

Hiding underneath my covers,
Afraid of nighttime stirring,
This World full of terrors
Starts my fear a whirring.
I made a crafty plan,
Thought up just today.
Send letters to each monster
And this is what I'll say:
To all of the werewolves
And Mr. Spring Heel Jack,
Don't wake me with your noise.
I'm not a tasty snack.
Dr. Frankenstein and Monster,
This letter's just for you.
Don't come into my house,
Instead go to the zoo.
Those in Bran Castle
And all ye Vampires there,
Please, stay in Carpathia.
I hear it's nicer there.

These missives were mistakes.
Mailed out, but what comes next?
I sent them my address!
I should have sent a text.

Deep In the Woods
Joy Yin

I hiked down the trail,
Deeper and deeper into the woods.

I loved being in these woods,
But never had I ever
Been so deep down the trail before.

Still, I kept going.
I glanced down at my feet:
The trail was gone.
No trace.

As I panicked,
I was met by
The smell of gingerbread and peppermints,
Paired with the aura of the pines.
It felt like Christmas.

Unbeknownst to me,
I walked on.
My mind was foggy.
My consciousness, blurry.

The trees thickened.
The ground beneath me
Grew rocky and rigid.
It was hard to keep moving,
But I did.

Crows croaked
A bass warning.
Beware, beware!
But I didn't care.

In the shadows, a gingerbread cottage
Covered with giant peppermints lurked.
Smoke floated out of a little chimney.
A scent of chocolate chip cookies
Pulled me in.

My feet went closer.
Slowly,
I chipped off a piece
Of the gingerbread cottage.

It was surprisingly warm.
Just out of the oven.
Bit by bite
My chunk of the house
Disappeared.

As I was munching,
A hushed voice
Drifted through the smoke
And settled over me.

Dear,
Care to come inside
For tea?

Terror washed over me
Even as my feet slowly turned.

EARTH and SKY
Zeeshan Shahzad

In a world where beauty is discovered,
The story of earth and sky is told.
The earth, tender cradle of life,
The sky, the canvas on which dreams flourish.

Beneath the emerald green of the earth lies
A carpet of invisible wonders.
The majestic mountains rise into the sky
As the rivers dance and the birds fly.

The earth breathes life in every season,
The flowers that bloom, a living ground.
From the smallest seed to the largest tree,
Nature's symphony whispers in the wind.

But up there the sky rises and paints
The colors of day and night.
An unprecedented masterpiece
In shades of orange, pink, and blue.

Together they form a harmonious fusion,
A heavenly dance that never ends.
For earth and heaven, forever joined,
A truly divine partnership.

Let us therefore nurture this precious bond
By lovingly tending the beauty of the earth.
And as we gaze into the infinite sky,

Let our spirits soar and reach new heights.

Because in the union of earth and sky,
We find hope, joy, and reasons
To protect and love this planet we share,
A home so sacred and incomparable.

Webs
Elizabeth Suggs

A spider claws up my throat
Its long legs floss through my teeth.
When I speak, it steals my voice.
This thing keeps me trapped,
forever expanding upward,
Webbing through my mind.
Soon there will only be the void of thought—
The emptiness of matter,
Drifting in space,
Me and you perpetually tangled as one.

Tenebrism
Talysa Sainz

The shop was unremarkable—
mostly crystals and herbs
to cover the inadequate pay
of tarot readings.
The witch was best known
for the gorgeous paintings she sold,
full of radiant colors
and shady subject matter.
But Misty put her best work
into the art she kept to herself.

She pricked her finger
and let the droplets fall
into her paint jars
of varying sizes
glowing along the windowsill.
She dipped her brush
into the glossy black,
swirled it around,
and let the color melt
onto the canvas.

Misty learned this trick from her
grandmother—the magic blood
skipped a generation.
"Bleed into the painting," she said,
"and bring your art to life."
She focused on her subject

the "accidental" death
of her main competitor
the fake witch lording over
the shop down the street.

Flickering candles cast long shadows
mingling with the soft silhouette
created by the fading sunset
out the window.
She tried to mimic the shadows
in her masterpiece.
The tenebrism struck the heart
in a peculiar way,
the stark juxtaposition
of light and dark, touching.

The more somber the content,
the brighter the colors
she tended to use—
create a balance between
the light and darkness.
The stronger the contrast,
the intensity,
the brilliance
in her artwork,
the faster the magic worked.

Sundown, A Beginners Guide to Delirium
Greg R. Goodman

In the quiet hours of dusk,
fatigue, that pernicious prankster,
casts shadows of doubt
across the mental landscape.
When isolated in this twilight of the infinite,
the sleepy mind distorts the subtle boundary layer
between the real and what is illusion.

Peering into this obscurity, specters are perceived,
surreptitiously in transition along the margin.
These apparitions are gradually fixed in thought
and like a developing photograph comes into clarity—
the phantoms are realized.
Vigilance is required to avoid their mayhem,
but lassitude, an unyielding nemesis,
grays the vision, allowing darkness
to swallow the surrounding space.

A sense of disorder follows,
like the wake of a body disturbing
the still night air nearby.
There is the feeling of moisture
from whispered words pressed close against the ear.
Then, the startled shiver of momentary panic,
as cold fingers drift across the throat
silencing the scream, before the body
is plundered of life.

Something Not Hopeless
Lillian Angelovic

I do not yet choose to give up all hope
Still grasping for its invisible strength
My own demons bind me tight without rope

Doubting thoughts rip at bright dreams, interloped
In silent explosions they claw and fang
Broken but crawling, I can't give up hope

Bright words splash in through my kaleidoscope
Images wished, twirling faith down its length
Still dark demons bind me tight without rope

Recurring winds loosen this thin tightrope
Unbalanced, eyes veiled and miserable hang
I must not let go and give up all hope

Bitter thoughts licked off an old envelope
Inside the letter, sweet memories up sang
My demons yet bind me down without rope

Remembered words lift, but age as I grope
List'ning, I bury my dream where it sprang
I do not yet choose to give up all hope
My own demons bind me tight without rope

Mermaids
Brian Mealing

The mermaids are singing.
I hear them.
Their voices are gold.
Like a dwarf, I chase the treasure,
But the gold crumbles.
I see Mermaids,
With sharp teeth
And fish faces.
They carry tridents;
Spear me like prey.
Leave only bones.

Common Cuckoo
Kevin Wasden

I am a common cuckoo
   Destructive and deceitful,
      Blameless by nature.

My father and his family
   They think me theirs
      In spite of my stature,
         In spite of my paleness,
            Despite the prudence in my eyes.

The truth in my blood
   Disconnects me--
      Twice a bastard child.
That which I hold is not mine,
And that which is mine I've never known.

The Stone Ruins of Mansion Madthena

Jonathan Reddoch

Beyond the realm of reason
Passed the crypt of forgotten knowledge
Through the fields where only dead roses grow
In the valley where snow refuses to fall

Lay the foundations ancient
Of the stately Mansion Madthena
Burned by hellfire to the core
Crumbled elegance and masonry

All that remains
Are the mounds of ashes
Archaic runes upon scorched bone
And the echoes of laughing mages and crying babes

About Lillian Angelovic

Lillian Angelovic writes award-winning poetry and fiction, and secretly edits every word she can get her hands on. She has a bachelor's degree in Broadcast Journalism, produces a popular faith-related leadership podcast, and helps recruit awesome people as hospital volunteers. Lillian lives in North Salt Lake, Utah, with her favorite movie partner, a crybaby cat, and a small forest of houseplants.

Poetry in this collection:
Funeral Tolling
I Was Troubled
Messy Leavings
Something Not Hopeless

About Skye Caden

Skye Caden is an avid reader and writer. Skye enjoys writing poetry and short fiction. When not writing, Skye's other interests and hobbies include entomology and political science. Skye's goals include a career in research ethnobiology and political activism. Skye is a member of the Horror Writers Association.

Poetry in this collection:
    House of the Fundead

About Linda M. Crate

Linda M. Crate's poetry, short stories, articles, and reviews have been published in a myriad of magazines both online and in print. She has twelve published chapbooks: A Mermaid Crashing Into Dawn (Fowlpox Press - June 2013), Less Than A Man (The Camel Saloon - January 2014), If Tomorrow Never Comes (Scars Publications, August 2016), My Wings Were Made to Fly (Flutter Press, September 2017), splintered with terror (Scars Publications, January 2018), More Than Bone Music (Clare Songbirds Publishing House, March 2019), the samurai (Yellow Arrowing Publishing, October 2020), Follow the Black Raven (Alien Buddha Publishing, July 2021), Unleashing the Archers (Guerilla Genesis Press, August 2021), Hecate's Child (Alien Buddha Publishing, November 2021) fat & pretty (Dancing Girl Press, June 2022), and searching stained glass windows for an answer (Alien Buddha Press, December 2022), and four micro poetry chapbooks. She is also the author of the novella Mates (Alien Buddha Publishing, March 2022). She also published her debut photography collection *Songs of the Creek* (Alien Buddha Press, April 2023) in spring of 2023.

Poetry in this collection:
Flaming Wings of Dreams

About K. Scott Forman

K. Scott Forman is the author of several short stories and poems, some appearing in his latest book, Lovecraft's Pillow and Other Weird Tales. He holds a Master of Fine Arts degree from the Jack Kerouac School of Disembodied Poetics at Naropa University, is a member of the Horror Writers Association, and tries to be a full-time writer when he's not being Mr. Mom. He enjoys sunsets with blood in them, long walks in inclement weather, and the Mark II line up of Deep Purple at volumes determined unsafe by the Surgeon General. He is currently at work on his first guitar recording and a middle grade fantasy novel.

Find him at kscottforman.com.

Poetry in this collection:
A Gravestone

About Greg R. Goodman

Although there is nothing as poetic as a well sewn anastomosis between blood vessels, words from the heart can more broadly touch the universal fabric of humanity. Greg, a retired, vascular surgeon, is re-orienting away from the science of medicine into the art of new directions. As a life-long learner, exploring new poetic horizons, both mentally and physically, remains high on his life's list of achievement.

Poetry in this collection:
Grave Thinking
Sundown, A Beginner's Guide to Delirium
The Mirror Cracked
The Stalking

About David C. Kopaska-Merkel

David C. Kopaska-Merkel, a semi-retired geologist, won the 2006 Rhysling award for best long poem (for a collaboration with Kendall Evans), and edits *Dreams & Nightmares* magazine (since 1986). He has edited *Star*line*, an issue of *Eye To The Telescope*, and several *Rhysling* anthologies, co-edited the 2023 *Dwarf Stars* anthology, has served as SFPA president, and is an SFPA Grandmaster. His poems have been published in *Asimov's*, *Analog*, *Strange Horizons*, and more than 200 other venues. His latest collection, **Some Disassembly Required**, winner of the Elgin award, was published by Diminuendo Press in 2022.

Blog: https://dreamsandnightmaresmagazine.blogspot.com/

Poetry in this collection:

Jack Rises

The Swimmer's Bones

(Note: These poems are untitled. The first lines were used as titles to facilitate chapter headings.)

About C.R. Langille

C.R. Langille spent many a Saturday afternoon watching monster movies with her mom. It wasn't long before she started crafting nightmares to share with her readers. She is a retired, disabled veteran with a deep love for weird and creepy tales. This prompted her to form Timber Ghost Press in January of 2021. She is an affiliate member of the Horror Writer's Association, the DEI Chair for the League of Utah Writers, and she received her MFA: Writing Popular Fiction from Seton Hill University in 2014.

Follow her here: https://link.heropost.io/crlangille

Poetry in this collection:
Branches and Bone
Siren's Sorrow

C. H. Lindsay (Charlie) is an award-winning poet & writer, housewife, and book-lover—not necessarily in that order. She currently has short stories and poetry in forty anthologies and magazines, including *Amazing Stories*, *Fantasy Magazine*, *Moonletters*, *Space and Time Magazine*, *Strange Horizons*, and *Utah's Best Poetry and Prose*. She is currently working on five novels, six short stories, and at least two dozen poems (although the numbers are always in flux).

In 2018 she became Al Carlisle's literary executor. She now publishes his true crime under *Carlisle Legacy Books, LLC.*

She is a member of SFWA, HWA, SFPA, LUW, and is a founding member of the Utah Chapter of the Horror Writers Association. Mostly blind, she lives in Utah with her "seeing-eye husband," library of books, and a bossy cat.

You can learn more about her at https://www.chlindsay.net.

Poetry in this collection:
    Aftermath
    Devolving to Grayscale
    Godless Society

About Inna Lyon

Inna Valerie Lyon is a Russian bumpkin raised on a steady diet of cabbage and potatoes peppered with the required reading of Chekhov and Dostoevsky.

During the day, Inna works as an accountant and specializes in producing colorful aging reports and cute collection letters.

At night, she writes stories about life, miracles, and cats.

Inna is a member of the League of Utah Writers, Blue Quill, and Infinite Monkeys chapters. She has a few writing awards for her essays and stories in different genres. She writes in both languages, English and Russian.

Inna lives in Utah with a big happy family.

Poetry in this collection:
I'm Forty-Fifth

About Brian Mealing

Brian Mealing loves to write poetry, often inspired by fairy tales and horror. He also loves comics, sci-fi, and other fandoms. He is a member of the Horror Writers Association. Brian lives in the scenic Rocky Mountains, where he curses each snowfall awaiting the warm summer.

Poetry in this collection:
Devour Like Sharks
Mermaids

About Jonathan Reddoch

Jonathan Reddoch is co-owner of Collective Tales Publishing. He is a father, writer, editor, and publisher. He writes sci-fi, fantasy, romance, and especially horror. He has been working on his enormous sci-fi novel for over a decade and would like to finish it in this lifetime if possible.

Poetry in this collection:
Comfort to Know
Sophie's Lantern
The Divine Crow
The Stone Ruins of Mansion Madthena

About Talysa Sainz

Talysa Sainz is a freelance editor and award-winning author who believes life's deepest truths can be found in fiction. She runs her own editing business and spends her time at the library or volunteering with the League of Utah Writers. Always fascinated with the structure of words, she studied English Linguistics and Editing at BYU. She then went on to receive a Master of Science in Management and Leadership, focusing on nonprofit work, from WGU. Talysa is the President of the Utah Freelance Editors.

Poetry in this collection:
Nebrit
Tenebrism

About Zeeshan Shahzad

Zeeshan Shahzad is a poet, short story writer, and scriptwriter from Pakistan.

Poetry in this collection:
>Autumn Autumn
>EARTH and SKY

About Joshua P. Sorensen

Joshua P. Sorensen is from Orem, Utah (United States). He travels extensively, inspiring him to write poetry and short fiction (mostly horror). His other loves include history, nature, and all things geek. Joshua is a member of the Horror Writers Association and the League of Utah Writers. He can be found on Amazon:

amazon.com/author/joshuapsorensen

Poetry in this collection:
My Undead Neighbor
Penpals?
The Ghost of My Room

About Elizabeth Suggs

Elizabeth Suggs is a multifaceted personality entrenched in the world of literature and creative pursuits. As the co-owner of Collective Tales Publishing and the proprietor of Editing Mee, she commands a prominent position in the realm of indie publishing. Her creative prowess extends to her role as an accomplished author, credited with crafting numerous award-winning stories. Notably, one of her tales attained Amazon Bestseller collection, solidifying her standing in the literary domain. Beyond her roles in publishing and writing, Elizabeth wears the hat of a discerning book reviewer on EditingMee.com and captivates audiences as a celebrated bookstagramer and cosplayer under the moniker @ElizabethSuggsAuthor. Despite her immersive involvement in the literary world, she finds joy in other pursuits, indulging in video and board games, as well as showcasing her culinary talents by baking delightful cookies. Elizabeth Suggs embodies a vibrant blend of creativity and passion across various facets of her life.

Poetry in this collection:
Sentiments and Snacks
Webs

About Kevin Wasden

Kevin Wasden's creative journey weaves through the realms of art, writing, and education. He earned his bachelor's degree at Utah State University, where his academic focus spanned visual arts, creative writing, and social sciences. Furthering his educational endeavors, he completed his Master of Education at Southern Utah University. Kevin's literary footprint extends across a diverse range of works, including the Hazzardous Universe book series (2011 and 2012), CulturED: Pathways to Meaningful School Change (2022), Lost Between Light & Shadow: A Collection of Dark Poetry (2024), and Dog Save the King: An LTUE Benefit Anthology (2025).

Poetry in this collection:
Common Cuckoo
The Leviathan
The Rocking Horse

About Joy Yin

Joy Yin is a writer, poet, and artist from Wuhan, China, though she has lived in California for 5 years. She is fluent in Mandarin and English but also learning Spanish. Joy has always had a love for reading and writing. As of now, she has works either forthcoming or already published in Skipping Stones Magazine, Scfaikuest, the new Drabbun Anthology (Hiraeth Books), Cold Moon Journal, Triya, Star*Line, and more. She's currently 13 years old and attending an international school in Mexico City. Right now, she's working on a collection of micro-poetry. In her free time, she likes to curl up and read a good book (however, she doesn't quite like rereading).

Poetry in this collection:
Deep In the Woods

Publisher's Note

While this book is subtitled "A collection of dark poetry," the place between light and shadow is often filled with both.

Similarly, these poems contain a variety of themes that go from light to dark and the places in between.

It is suitable for a wide range of readers. I hope each of you find something that resonates with you or sparks your imagination.

I've been considering putting together a poetry collection for several years, but it didn't come together until a discussion last year during a meeting of the Utah Chapter of the Horror Writers Association. I am grateful to them for their encouragement and support.

Special thanks go to Joshua P. Sorensen and Daniel Cureton for their help with the selection process.